WITHDRAWN

D1644383

What Faust Saw

PERTH & KINROSS COUNCIL

05678113

FOR JACQUELINE

First published in Ireland and Britain in 1997
by Wolfhound Press
68 Mountjoy Square, Dublin 1, Ireland.
First published in Australia and New Zealand in 1995
by Hodder Headline Australia Pty Limited
(A member of the Hodder Headline Group)
10-16 South Street, Rydalmere NSW 2116, Australia

Copyright © Matthew Ottley 1995

All rights reserved. No part of this book may be reproduced or utilised in any form or by any means electronic,
digital or mechanical including photography, filming, recording, video recording, photocopying,
or by any information storage and retrieval system or shall not, by way of trade or otherwise, be lent,
resold or otherwise circulated in any form of binding or cover other than that in which it is published
without prior permission in writing from the publisher.

Wolfhound Press receives financial assistance from the Arts Council/
An Chomhairle Ealaíon, Dublin.

British Library Cataloguing in Publication Data
A catalogue record for this book is available from the British Library

ISBN 0-86327-603-2

Designed by Liz Seymour
Printed in Hong Kong

What Faust Saw

MATT OTTLEY

WOLFHOUND PRESS

One night Faust woke up, looked out the window and ...

... saw something *very* strange.

He tried to wake up Mum … **and** Isabelle … **and** Clayton …

...*even* Dad.

But they didn't seem to want to WAKE UP.

Faust hid.

Faust HOWLED!

That woke up Dad.

But he couldn't see anything strange.

'Bad dog!' said Dad.

He locked Faust outside.

Poor Faust.

Soon he was back inside.

'Bad, **bad** dog!'

said Mum.

'Outside again!'

'Bad, bad, bad, bad, bad dog!'

said Dad **and** Mum **and** Isabelle **and** Clayton.

Now **Faust** was getting **ANGRY**.

It wasn't *his* fault.

He decided to *run away.*
Then they'd be sorry.

But he was followed...

Faust FLED.

But he was tired.

After all he hadn't had much sleep.

The next morning Dad *and* Mum *and* Isabelle *and* Clayton came to the pound.

EXHIBITION

LIFE ON OTHER PLANETS

MUSE

Faust decided to forgive them and go home.

He also decided that the next time he woke up and saw something strange ...

...he would go back to sleep.